Richard Paul Evans

The Dance

Illustrations by
Jonathan Linton

All of the author's proceeds from this book will
go to help abused and neglected children.

Simon & Schuster Books for Young Readers

To my daughters, who dance my heart

—R. P. E.

To my wife, Julie. Love, Jonathan

—J. L.

Author's Acknowledgments

I wish to acknowledge those who made this book possible: Jonathan Linton and his wife, Julie; Jed Platt; Laurie Liss; Les Morgenstein; Ann Brashares; Rick Richter; Stephanie Lurie; and all those at S&S children's division. Most of all, thanks be to the source of all inspiration, love, and light.

—R. P. E.

Artist's Acknowledgments

I wish to thank the many people who helped with this project and most especially Jed Platt, for starting it all. My special thanks to Tawna Spoor, Lisa May, and Brandi Anderson for keeping it all going. To Lizzy, Abigail, Allyson, Jenna, Cameron, Jim, Rebecca, and Jana, my great models, and to Skip, for being a great model and support. To Ron and Kristy Huber for their time and dedication. To my wonderful family, especially my mom and dad, and, of course, Julie. And finally, the Evans family and Rick, for his trust, his encouragement, his vision, and his friendship.

—J. L.

SIMON & SCHUSTER BOOKS FOR YOUNG READERS
An imprint of Simon & Schuster Children's Publishing Division
1230 Avenue of the Americas, New York, New York 10020
Text copyright © 1999 by Richard Paul Evans
Illustrations copyright © 1999 by Jonathan Linton
All rights reserved including the right of reproduction in whole or in part in any form.
Simon and Schuster Books for Young Readers is a trademark of Simon and Schuster.
Book design by Edward Miller
The text of this book is set in 20-pt. Centaur.
The illustrations are rendered in oil paint.
Printed in the United States of America
ISBN 0-689-82351-7

Produced by 17th Street Productions,
a division of Daniel Weiss Associates, Inc.
33 West 17th Street, New York, NY 10011

Author's Note

In the process of creating *The Dance*, a print of the image of the little girl on the cover was sent to me by a friend. I was captivated by the painting. It was as though the artist, Jonathan Linton, had borrowed from the very images of my imagination. Even though we had already commissioned another talented artist, I felt that Jonathan Linton should be hired and that very painting used.

I learned that the picture was a private commission painted years before from a photograph of a little girl named Lizzy Brooks. I also learned that the previous summer, Lizzy and her mother had been killed in a car accident. Haunted by the image of the little girl and aware of the sensitive nature of sharing such an image, I contacted the girl's father, Skip Brooks, about the possibility of using the painting. He graciously agreed, as a way to preserve and share his daughter's light and joy. He had only one request—that I share in this book a poem he had written to his wife and daughter. It is with deep appreciation and admiration that I do so.

> *I have two angels that abide with me. And where I go, they go. And what I feel They know — and what I know they sense. When they dance, we see. For the Music transcends the Veil that brings into the light, the image of their souls and All their glory. Because they have hearts that moved before us . . . And know and feel the joy and wonder Of His loving ways. I have two angels, two of the sweetest angels, that abide with me. It is His way. Two by Two.*
>
> *They need not wait for me in the garden deep, for the garden blooms within. Where the soil light spreads its way with light before its path where all can see and sense it is so. How do I know, you ask? Can this be true? I have two angels, for they abide with me. For it is my light they see, and know it is me. It is their light I know that abides with me.* —Skip Brooks

A father once had a daughter.

She was a happy little girl who liked the things that little girls do—dress-ups and kittens and sometimes both together.

But most of all she liked to dance.

Nearly every day she would jump and spin
in the thick wild grass near the edge of the yard
where the tall meadow flowers grew.

Though she didn't see him, her father watched.

And he smiled.

When the girl was old enough to go to school she danced in the Thanksgiving play, dressed as an ear of corn. She could not see out of her costume very well and tripped over a boy dressed as a carrot.

Though she could not see her father, he was watching.

And he smiled.

When the girl was a little older, she took dancing lessons. She wore a pink tutu and soft leather ballet slippers. At her first dance recital she tried very hard to remember her steps. She did not see her father standing close to the stage.

But he was smiling.

A few years later the girl became a graceful ballerina. She wore pink satin toe shoes with long shiny ribbons. One year she danced a solo in *The Nutcracker.* Everyone clapped when she finished. The crowd was large and the stage lights were bright so the girl could not see her father in the audience. But he clapped louder than anyone else.

And he smiled wider than anyone else.

The girl grew into a young woman. One spring night she put on a beautiful gown and high-heeled pumps and went to her first prom with a young man.

When the young man brought her home, they did not see her father peeking out the window as they slow-danced on the front porch.

(He wasn't smiling.)

The young woman fell in love with the young man and they soon decided to marry. At the end of the wedding day she waltzed with her father. Then the father gave his girl's hand to the young man and left the dance floor. As the young woman gazed into her new husband's eyes she did not see her father watching from the side of the room.

Though the father's eyes were moist, he smiled.

The young woman and her new husband moved far away from the home with the thick grass and tall meadow flowers.

Whenever he missed his daughter, the father would take out an old shoe box filled with photographs of her dancing. As he looked at the pictures, he remembered each dance.

And he smiled.

Many years passed.

One day the father called his daughter on the telephone. "I am old now. I am cold and very tired," he said. "Please come to me. I would like to see you dance just one more time."

The daughter came. She found her father in his bed. And she danced for him.

But the father did not smile.

"I cannot see you," he said. "My eyes are not much good. Dance close to the bed so that I can hear your feet."

The woman walked close to the bed, then she jumped and spun as she had as a little girl.

The father smiled.

Then the woman sat on her father's bed.

She lay her face against his, took his hand, and they swayed back and forth. In this way, they danced once more.

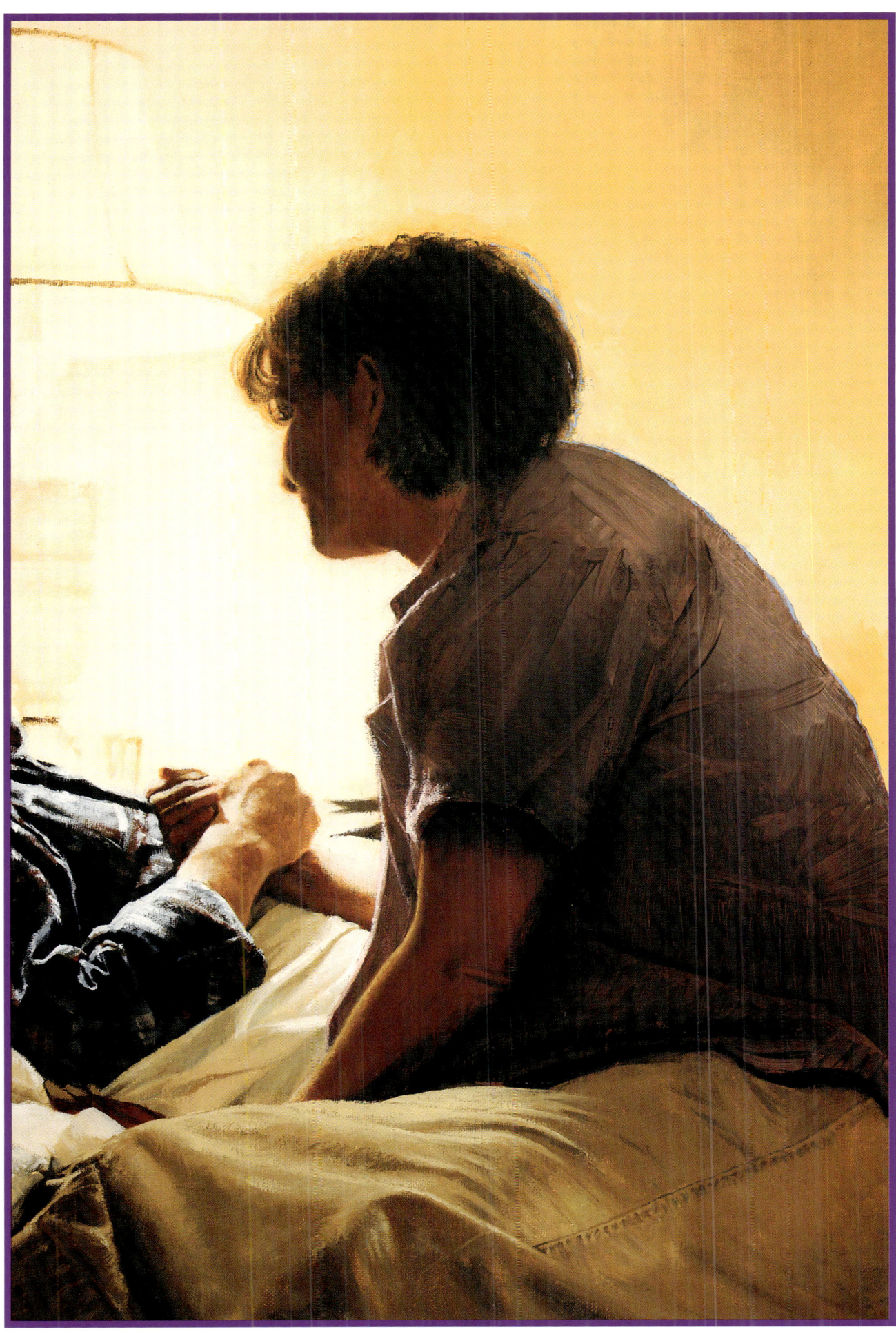

"I have danced many times," the woman whispered into her father's ear, "in many places and for many people. But I have always danced for you. How can I ever dance again?" She buried her head in her father's chest.

But her father shook his head.

"You must never stop dancing," he said. "For though you will not see me, whenever you dance, I will be watching."

Then the father went to sleep.

As the daughter sadly left his side, she stopped at the doorway and looked back once more at the father she loved.

And then she danced.

And though she could not see him, her father was watching.

And he smiled.